Mem Fox

A Particular Cow

Illustrated by
Terry Denton

Harcourt, Inc.
Orlando   Austin   New York   San Diego   Toronto   London

www.HarcourtBooks.com

Library of Congress Cataloging-in-Publication Data
Fox, Mem, 1946–
A particular cow/Mem Fox; illustrated by Terry Denton.
p.   cm.
Summary: A particular cow has some particularly unusual
adventures on a particular Saturday morning.
[1. Cows–Fiction.]   I. Denton, Terry, ill.   II. Title.
PZ7.F8373Pa   2006
[E]–dc22   2004030060
ISBN-13: 978-0-15-200250-3   ISBN-10: 0-15-200250-2

First edition

A C E G H F D B

Printed in Singapore

The illustrations in this book were done
in black ink and watercolor on Arches paper.
The display type and text type were set in Handwriter.
Color separations by Bright Arts Ltd., Hong Kong
Printed and bound by Tien Wah Press, Singapore
This book was printed on totally chlorine-free
Stora Enso Matte paper.
Production supervision by Jane Van Gelder
Designed by Lauren Rille

For Terry Denton,
a particular hero—M.F.

For Evie, who went
for a particular walk—T.D.

Every Saturday morning a particular cow
went for a particular walk.

Usually nothing particular happened.

Until one particular Saturday when
she found herself on the wrong side
of a particular pair of bloomers...

and a particular woman...

and a particular postman...

and a particular party of children...

and a particular bridegroom...

and a particular gang of sailors,

who almost sank in a particular river

on account of this particular cow
that we're talking about,

tossed her tail at the summer flies,

and went on her way without surprise,

on that particular Saturday morning.